Coffee Shop Christmas is dedicated to our Police Officers, who put their lives on the line daily.
Thank you for your service!
And
To the Lord Jesus Christ, Who gave His Life on the cross for our Salvation.
Thank You for Your Sacrifice!

Contents

Acknowledgements 5

Introduction 6

Characters of Importance 7

Chapter One: Those Sirens 8

Chapter Two: Katherine's Request 15

Chapter Three: Winter Wonderland 23

Chapter Four: The Writer 27

Chapter Five: Wounded Spirit 35

Chapter Six: Career Girl 41

Chapter Seven: Deep Wounds 49

Chapter Eight: Others First 59

Chapter Nine: Saying Goodbye 65

Chapter Ten: Merry Christmas 73

My Testimony 78

Other Books By Ryana Lynn! 79

Acknowledgements

First, I would like to thank the Lord for giving me the idea for this story and guiding me through the drafts, edits and publication of this project. Thank You for all Your Blessings!

Secondly, I'd like to thank my family again for all of their help! It couldn't have been done without y'all! Thanks so much!

My editing team has been amazing! Thanks, Mom (for proofing and editing assistance), Grandpa Miller (for grammatical checking) and Gera (for Beta-Reading).

And the amazing cover design! Thank you so much, Gera, for making this the most amazing cover I could ever have hoped for!

I'd also like to thank Victoria Minks for her article on Color Coded Editing, which made my edits so much easier! Thank you for being my writing buddy, even though you are on the other side of the world!

A big "thank you" goes to our Police Officers for all they do to keep us safe, day and night. From the bottom of my heart, Thank you and God Bless you!

Introduction

I thank God we have First Responders who are willing to put their lives on the line for us every single day. This book is my tribute to one group of Responders, our Police Force.

When planning this book, I had no idea violence against our Policemen would escalate the way it has now. I couldn't believe it when I pulled out my sketches and realized how this book lined up with the times.

I thank God that every day, around the clock, there are Policemen ready to protect and defend us on the home front, just as our servicemen do overseas.

As you read this story, I hope you like the quaint little coffee shop atmosphere I've tried to create. Pour yourself a cup of coffee, wrap up in a blanket, turn on some relaxing Christmas music, and enjoy *Coffee Shop Christmas*. Have fun and God Bless!

In Christ, Ryana Lynn

Characters of Importance

Katherine Shannon: Owner and operator of *The Coffee Shop*. Since the death of her husband the previous year, Katherine has managed to support herself with the shop, but finds her "real work" is encouraging others in her community.

Sgt. Dan Piper: Katherine's brother-in-law. Dan is a Police Officer who works across the street from *The Coffee Shop*. He frequents the establishment when work permits, often bringing a fellow officer to enjoy the warm, stress-free atmosphere.

Bella Cunningham: A young author who believes the only thing that matters in life is the perfect story.

Cpl. Justin Ericson: A Policeman from a neighboring town. Justin wants some peace and quiet, away from the constant accusations that accompany his job.

Nicole Hannover: She's got it all…a music scholarship and a chance to make it big in the world of concert pianists…but should she?

Chapter 1
Those Sirens

*And they that know thy name will put their trust in thee: for thou,
LORD, hast not forsaken them that seek thee.*
Psalm 9:10

The jingling of keys reached the ear of Deputy Ellis Wright. He smiled and hurried down the sidewalk.
"Good morning, Ms. Katherine!"
Katherine Shannon smiled at the young policeman.
"Good morning, Ellis."
"I'll check the place over for you this morning."
Katherine nodded and let Ellis in ahead of her. Someone from the station always checked the building over before she opened up. Special orders from her police officer brother-in-law Dan.
Ellis flipped on the lights and scanned the front room of the coffee shop. Finding no one, he proceeded to the kitchen and store room. He returned to the counter, where Katherine was unpacking her grocery bags. "No one here but us. Do you need anything?"
"No thank you, Ellis, I believe I can manage. You'll be stopping by later?"
"I think so, if they'll let me go. I-"

The no-nonsense voice of a dispatcher echoed from the scanner mounted on the counter of *The Coffee Shop*. Ellis was paged. Saying a hasty goodbye, he sprinted out the door and across the street.

Blue and red lights bounced off the walls as a patrol car pulled out of the police station parking lot moments later.

And then the sirens.

Katherine buried her face in her hands as the car sped off. Her lips trembled as she prayed aloud, "Lord, be with Dan and Ellis as they answer this call. Help them to stay calm and level headed."

Her breathing was unsteady. Her voice shook, betraying the tears welling up inside of her. "Protect them and bring them back safe. Please be with the ones who made the call. Keep them safe and let the situation be resolved quickly. Thy will be done, Father. In Jesus' name I pray, Amen."

Katherine glanced up at the clock on her wall, her intense blue eyes taking in the numbers, 5:15 am. It was Christmas Eve and Katherine soon had coffee brewed and ready for purchase. The deep scent of roasted grounds swirled through her small shop, mingling with sweet vanilla, spicy cinnamon and sugary baked apples. But even these comforting smells couldn't relax her.

Those sirens, she thought, brushing a wisp of chocolate brown hair behind her ear. Today, a year prior, she had heard about a convenience store robbery over the scanner. She heard her husband, Sgt. Bryson Shannon, respond that he would be heading right out. Knowing she had her scanner on at the house, he had said, "I love you, Katie!"

She blinked her eyes rapidly as she remembered the words… She didn't know that was the last time she would hear Bryson's voice.

She also recalled the text she had sent him, knowing his partner would read it to him. "I luv u, Bry ☺ B careful <3."

It hadn't been long after that when her brother-in-law, Sgt. Dan Piper, and her sister Isabelle had driven up to her

house in Dan's squad car. Dan had hurried her to the back seat and sped off for the hospital…
Katherine closed her eyes, trying to shut out more memories. Why torture herself? Bryson was gone now, spending another Christmas in Heaven. At least his partner had survived. There was no sense in rehashing the painful memories.
Ever since that day Katherine had purposed in her heart that, with God's help, she would not become bitter. It would only hurt worse. Besides, why should she begrudge her husband his promotion to Heaven, the only promotion he had ever really wanted? And one day she would join him.
The weeks and months following Bryson's death had been hard. Katherine found herself waiting up nights for Bryson to come home, only to realize he never would. Then she would relive the pain anew. She was all alone in that big empty house.
But grief wasn't her only foe. Katherine had been a homemaker all her life, and now she had to find a means of supporting herself. She and Bryson had never been blessed with children, though they had wanted them dearly. Cleaning her own house wouldn't put food on her table, and she didn't want to be a burden on her family. Surely there was something she could do to pay the bills!
It was Dan who had suggested she reopen the old coffee shop across the street from the police station. She was good at baking and making specialty coffee drinks…Bryson had always emphasized that fact to his co-workers. It seemed the perfect solution, and with a little help from Dan and Isabelle, the place had been obtained and fixed up.
The name was simple: *The Coffee Shop*. Straight to the point, just how Katherine liked it. As you entered the building, you could see the whole dining area. Three booths on the left and three on the right were perfect for business meetings of four or less. The four small tables in the middle space were usually taken by couples or single occupants. Six swivel seats

lined the long counter, which were the favorite perches for her police friends.

The decorations were warm and inviting. Katherine was a lover of vintage and country pieces, adding to the charm of the small structure. She had a section dedicated to the Police Force she loved and a Military display was across from it on the opposite wall. Nothing too big, but big enough.

It looked just right: down to earth and cozy.

A small tree was in the front window adorned with homemade coffee mug ornaments sprinkled among the Nativity ones. She had also added a few squad cars in tribute to her husband. Since it was Christmas, each table had a small Nativity centerpiece and a larger one was displayed on the counter.

The bell above the door jingled and Deputy Peter Cox walked in. He was one of the young men Bryson had been able to lead to the Lord before his death. Pulling herself out of her melancholy, Katherine forced a smile as he approached the counter. "Morning, Deputy Cox. What can I do for ya?"

"I'm in the mood for something different…how about the Peppermint Mocha?"

Katherine nodded. "Coming right up. That'll be $2.50."

"Alright…" Peter replied, counting out the money. "Do me a favor and don't tell the fellows I got a sweet coffee. They'll never let me live it down!" The two laughed as Katherine gave him his change.

As she fixed the warm drink, she asked, "How's Amy adjusting to our town?"

Peter's face lit up at the mention of his new wife. "She loves it! She misses her family of course, but she says our town's like stepping back into the 40's or 50's. At first, I thought she meant that as a put down, but then she told me she'd always dreamed of living in a town like this. It's large but has that small town feel. And she's in love with the library."

"Oh, yes. I know how she feels about the town and the library. I borrowed a new book from there, a WWII novel about the fall of Paris. I haven't finished it yet, but I'll let you know how it turns out."

Peter nodded eagerly. He loved reading historical novels when he had the chance, and his wife shared that love. He took the coffee Katherine handed him. "Amy said she wants me to bring her here when I get a day off. I've been talking about your coffee and your chocolate chip cookies. She wants to find out if your cookies are anything like her mother's."

Katherine laughed, beginning to relax. Talking to others helped the unpleasant memories of the previous year fade away. "You bring her and I'll give her one on the house as a welcome to the neighborhood. I'll look forward to the taste testing!"

Before long Peter took his leave, and Katherine was left once more to watch the officers coming and going from the station through her front window. Dan and Ellis were still out on their call. Again she prayed for their safety…and again past memories flooded her mind.

She hadn't been enthusiastic about entering the world of police officers when she and Bryson had first moved to the cozy town. Not that she didn't appreciate the force and their work; she was just looking forward to less stress once Bryson left the military…but God had other plans.

Katherine soon found that with her military wife experience, she was able to relate better to the other police wives and their families. She knew what it was like to stay awake late into the night waiting for the "Everything's alright, nothing to worry about" email, text or phone call. Many of the men on the force were younger than she and Bryson, so their families appreciated the understanding and advice from an experienced couple.

A smiled slowly made its way across her face. Katherine liked these warm, happy memories. She had become the "special aunt" to all the children born to the men at the station. They loved the new tradition of getting a free birthday cookie at *The Coffee Shop* and often sent pictures they had colored for her to hang up on her bulletin board.

Some boys on the force seemed to think of her as an aunt themselves. Special events were told to her, and certain trials were shared as well. She was honored that they would share their triumphs and trials with her.

Of course, these tough guys would never call it "sharing their trials"...they were too "cool" for that! But they knew Mrs. Shannon would always have a Bible verse or a story to share from her husband Bryson's experiences that always seemed to help.

Katherine's thoughts now went back to those first few months after Bryson's death. There wasn't a day that went by without one of the fellows stopping by her house, just to make sure she was alright. Sometimes they would bring their family over for a short visit or drop off a meal. They were just as supportive to her as her church and family. In fact, in a very special way, they *were* her family.

Katherine understood the potential danger these men faced every day and she took it seriously. What a tragedy it would be for one of these brave men to lose his life for all eternity while possibly saving another life!

This sense of urgency spurred Katherine to action. The tract rack on the counter always had plenty of material for her to hand out and small scripture plaques dotted the establishment. No, Katherine Shannon was not one of God's lazy laborers.

She wiped down the chalkboard menu that was normally propped up behind the counter. It was smudged and needed updating. She carefully wrote the season's specials on the board, as well as the old faithfuls.

Due to many requests, Salted Caramel Lattés had been added to the list, though Katherine personally wasn't crazy over them. But she did like the Peppermint Mochas. Mint Chocolate was a favorite of everyone who tried it, as well as her Home-style Hot Chocolate.

To add some zest to the same old classics, Katherine had renamed them. The Squad Car Special was simply a cup of coffee and a pastry of the customer's choice. It was a personal joke between her and her brother-in-law because of the age-old police-donut-coffee stereotype.

A laugh escaped her as she remembered Dan begging her not to carry donuts in her shop. "It'll only make the teasing worse!"

"You don't have to eat them, Dan," she had defended, for she personally liked homemade donuts.

"I never should have suggested you open this place," he mockingly lamented. She still remembered the look of "horror" on his face when he found out what The Squad Car Special was.

Just as she finished up her sign, a car pulled up outside the shop…a police car.

Chapter 2
Katherine's Request

Be careful for nothing; but in every thing by prayer and supplication with thanksgiving let your requests be made known unto God.
Philippians 4:6

Safe, Katherine sighed as Dan and Ellis entered the shop. Ellis appeared worn out and Katherine was sure his right eye was bruised. They greeted her and took their customary seats at the counter. They were grateful for a chance to sit and enjoy some coffee without having to rush off.

"Morning! Merry Christmas! What can I do for ya?" Katherine asked, trying to sound at ease, though Dan sensed the undercurrent of anxiety in her voice. And why not? Ellis' jaw was discolored and one eye was swollen. The twenty-three year old deputy was the same age as Katherine's youngest brother and she seemed especially protective of him.

"Same-ol'-same-ol'," Dan replied, glancing at Ellis, who was resting his head on his right hand.

Katherine nodded, a smile on her lips. "No doughnuts?"

"Stereotype-er!" Dan mumbled and Katherine laughed.

She turned to Ellis. "What about you?"

"As strange as this may sound," he began, wincing a little as he spoke, "I really want something cold. Do you serve

iced coffee in December?" he asked, his voice unnaturally low and quiet.
"Sure. Anything special or just plain iced coffee?"
"Uh…make it mocha," he murmured.
"Coming right up," she said.
Katherine peered back at Ellis, studying him. "Ellis, are you alright?"
Ellis glanced at Dan. Katherine's brother-in-law laughed slightly before answering for the young man, "He's doing as well as anyone can who's been socked twice in the face, once in the stomach and hasn't slept in 24 hours."
Katherine made a brisk turn at this announcement. "Oh, Ellis!" she exclaimed. "I'm so sorry! Do you need an ice pack? Of course you do. Here's your coffee, Dan, and your apple jack. I'll be right back," she called over her shoulder.
Ellis shook his head. "She's just like my mom. Well, my mom would actually make me lay on the couch with my feet up."
"*Make* you?" Dan questioned. Ellis narrowed his eyes.
Katherine retuned, still chattering. "Here's an ice pack, Ellis. I'll have your drink ready in a minute."
Ellis nodded then held his head as a loud *whrrrrrr* sound came from the kitchen. Katherine brought him his drink and sat across from the two policemen.
Ellis took a large gulp of his frozen drink. He worked his jaw a little and said, "Oh, that feels *soooo* good!"
"So what happened on the call?" Katherine asked, focusing on Ellis' bruised jaw. Her sisterly feelings were evident in her tone as she asked, "How did you get hurt, Ellis?"
"I'll answer your first question," Dan said. He took another bite of the apple pie-like pastry before continuing. "It was a breaking and entering over on North Street. Katie, you know where the Howes live, right? Well, it was the red house just past their place. It was a kid that called, and you know how nervous that can make a guy."

Katherine knit her brow and closed her eyes. "The poor child," she whispered, imagining the fear the young one must have been going through.

"When we got there, we could hear a man inside the house yelling for everybody to get down. More officers pulled up and secured the area, then I went inside. Ellis followed me."

Dan took a sip of his drink and Ellis picked up the story. "We found the intruder in the living room. Our backup men got the family out and Dan covered the guy while I went to disarm and handcuff him." Ellis shook his head. "I seriously believe that guy was a heavy weight boxing champ."

Dan explained, "He let Ellis have it three good times before we could get a hold of him. The backup guys took him out while I brought Ellis back to the 21st Century."

Katherine's hand went to her mouth. "He knocked you out?"

Ellis gave her a lopsided smile and nodded. "Yep, woke up with Dan shaking me and Cpl. Benson yelling for the Paramedics to 'get over here!'"

"So you have been checked out, Ellis?" Katherine confirmed. "You could have a concussion!"

Dan laughed. "He's in sound condition," he said, slapping his partner on the back. Ellis grimaced. "...if a bit bruised up. That's what took most of our time up there. The EMTs checked him out real good on site and said he would be A-Okay."

Katherine was satisfied with this information. "Any...did anyone...?"

The guys looked at each other, having a silent conversation. "Everybody is okay now," Dan said slowly. "The dad was injured before we got there, but he's fine. They took him to the hospital and they reported in that he's stable. Just a flesh wound."

Katherine let her breath out. "Thank God he's alright." She glanced over at Bryson's picture hanging on the wall. She turned back to Dan. "Did y'all ever find out what was going on the other day in Laneville?"

"Yes," Dan said with a nod. "They had an out and out anti-police riot over there. Thankfully, they were able to get it under control fairly quick, but there were a few shots fired."

"Anyone injured?" Katherine pressed.

Again, Dan and Ellis exchanged glances. "Yeah, but everyone's gonna be fine. There was a sergeant, a corporal and a rioter. The rioter was released from the hospital and transferred to jail. And the sergeant is still in the hospital, expected to be released next week."

Katherine shook her head. "In the hospital for Christmas. His poor family!" She squared her shoulders. "What about the corporal?"

"He was released from the hospital today," Dan replied. "I don't have details, but I do know they said he'd be limping for a while. And because of our dear friends, the media, he has been placed on administrative leave. About fifteen rioters are in custody."

"I see," Katherine whispered, her throat constricting her from being any louder.

Katherine looked at Ellis' swollen eye. "Would you like some pepperoni to put on that? I hear meat draws out the bruising."

Ellis grinned and Dan laughed heartily. "He's not a pizza, Katie! I've got to tell Isabelle this one! And I think doctors say now that meat on eyes isn't a good idea with all the hormones and stuff."

"Whatever you say, Sgt. Piper," Katherine replied, laughing too at her ridiculous suggestion.

Ellis just shook his head and smiled, then winced at the pain the muscle movement caused. His cellphone rang and he quickly answered it. "Hello…yeah, I'm at Katherine's shop with Dan…everything's fine…didn't you get my text?...I didn't send it? Honey, I'm so sorry! I thought I…what? Where are you?"

Katherine and Dan exchanged glances as Ellis listened to his wife's voice. "I'll get off as quick as I can! Just hang on, sweetheart, I'll meet you there!"

Ellis jumped to his feet as he ended the call. He grimaced as his stomach reminded him he shouldn't be jumping. "Kelly's in labor!" he exclaimed. He hurried toward the door, leaving the ice pack on the counter.

"Tell Kelly congrats for me!" Katherine called after him.

"Yes, ma'am, I sure will."

"Hey, Ellis!" Dan called. "Have Alex drive you to the hospital! You don't need to-" But Ellis was already gone, racing across the street to clock out, now wide awake.

Dan shook his head and paid for their drinks and breakfast. "I'd better go get Alex to give him a ride. I'll be back for lunch. You stay out of trouble," he teased.

"I'll try to refrain from robbing any banks," she responded with a grin. "Remember, y'all are to be at my place by 1:30 tomorrow, got it?"

He nodded and mentally filed away the information. "We'd never miss out on your roast beef and 'taters. That's all Jeff's been talking about," he said, referring to his ten year old son. "I'll see you later, Katie."

The bells jingled pleasantly as Dan left the building. Katherine turned to wipe off the counter when Dan stuck his head back inside. "Might want to turn up the heat. Looks like we're gonna have a white Christmas!"

"Sounds good to me!" Katherine said. She loved having snow for Christmas, which wasn't common in her area. Dan went back out and closed the door.

Katherine turned her attention to some dusting. The radio in the corner was turned down, but with the absence of voices, its soft strains reached her ears. *In the Bleak Midwinter*...one of her favorite songs...so relaxing and peaceful...jubilant with an undercurrent of sobriety.

She was about to start dusting some decorations when her stomach growled. She smiled. Time for her own breakfast.

Moments later, Katherine was settled behind the counter with a fresh French Vanilla Coffee and a warm apple jack. After blessing her meal, she took a bite of the delicious

cinnamon apple treat, allowing the flavors to take over her senses.
     She picked up the book she had borrowed from the library, *The Day She Fell*, about the fall of Paris back in the 1940's. This chapter jumped right into the action.
     It was a perfectly executed evil, this brilliantly wicked scheme of the German Third Reich. Madeline never suspected on that morning, which had begun so perfectly, her entire world would come crashing down around her...literally. Nor did she envision herself as a fugitive in her own home...
     Katherine had read four chapters before she pushed the book aside. The story was brilliant. Madeline was the main character, of course, and in one chapter everything she loved had been ripped away; her husband, home, and freedoms. She had watched as her husband was taken away by the Germans to some unknown fate...possibly to his death.
     Katherine could read no further. She had never lost her home or the freedom to walk down the street when she wanted, but she felt as though her husband had been ripped away from her. She had been robbed of many more years with Bryson; robbed of a proper goodbye.
     She fiercely fought back tears. She could see him, lying on a white hospital bed, wires and tubes and monitors all around him...and blood from his multiple injuries. She could hear his gasping breaths and feel the final squeeze he gave her hand before closing his eyes forever.
     In a way, Katherine envied Madeline. At least this fictional character had the hope of one day seeing her Henri again. She didn't *know* he was dead. But Katherine *knew* Bryson was gone.
     The author of that book is compelling, Katherine thought as she wiped her eyes. *Here I am blubbering over someone who doesn't even exist! How foolish! But, oh, Bryson!* She at last succumbed to the tears, her heart breaking once again.
     Katherine sighed and tried to pull herself together. Her heart skipped a beat as she looked at the clock. It was nearly

7:30 already. That was about the time Bryson had been sent out on that dreadful call that had resulted in his death.

"Stop feeling sorry for yourself, Katherine Shannon!" she scolded herself as she stood to check on some baked goods in the oven. "God gave Bryson to you for sixteen years of marriage. You should be grateful for that at least!"

Time ticked on as Katherine baked the day's pastries and tended customers. Several members of the police force dropped in for their favorite coffees and baked goods.

A few asked how she was doing, knowing it was the one year anniversary. Katherine replied that God's grace was sufficient.

She couldn't pretend she wasn't still grieving, but God truly was her strength. He had never left her nor forsaken her and she knew He never would. And He certainly knew she needed a double helping of His strength to get through today.

When the breakfast traffic was over, Katherine washed up some dishes in the back. She remained on the verge of tears and the pain of missing Bryson was nearly impossible to bear.

Lord, she cried out in her heart, *help me through another Christmas without Bryson. It's not easy! Father, sometimes I think I'll just die from missing him so much.*

A quiet sob escaped her once more. *You are my strength, but sometimes I need to be reminded. Last Christmas was hard, and I don't want to spend today and tomorrow making people feel sorry for me or by being depressed. Christmas is meant to be a happy time, celebrating Your birth...*

She took a deep breath and rinsed some cups. *Lord, why have You put me here? Why didn't You allow me to go back home? Why do I have to be around all the conflict and violence everyday? Am I right in staying here? Should I have opened the shop? Was that Your will or was I just following Dan's idea and my own desires, Lord? If I am supposed to be here, then please show me. Give me something to do for You that will give me assurance that You put me here. In Jesus' precious name I pray, Amen.*

As she finished her dishes, the music out front came to an abrupt stop...and the squealing of a weather alert blared through the shop.

Chapter 3
Winter Wonderland

Hast thou entered into the treasures of the snow? or hast thou seen the treasures of the hail,
Job 38:22

Katherine rushed to the front of her shop as the weather forecaster's voice announced, "The National Weather Service has detected a blizzard system moving towards the Springdale County area. A blizzard warning is in effect for the following towns: Bluefield, Davis, Harvey..."

Katherine let her breath out slowly as the warning towns were called out. Caudwell wasn't one of them. But heavy snow could be expected since they were on the outskirts of the storm bands.

She returned to the kitchen to put on some soup. With the cold weather, and the lunch hour approaching, she expected an influx of soup and sandwich sales.

Before long, the pleasant scent of hearty broccoli cheddar soup filled the kitchen. There was also a pot of broccoli pepper jack soup. That was a special request of the policemen that frequented during lunch.

Working quickly, Katherine made up some turkey sandwiches and placed them in the oven to keep warm. She checked her refrigerator to make sure she had mayonnaise, mustard, lettuce and cheese. That way she could customize the combos when the orders came.

Katherine could see snow already accumulating. Shivering, she turned up the heat on the thermostat.

The door opened and yet another policeman walked in. Chad Zane came at 11:45 everyday he was on duty, just like clockwork. Katherine grinned and called over her shoulder, "The usual?"

Chad nodded and sat at the counter. "You know I'm leery of new stuff."

She handed him his coffee and a chocolate chip cookie. "You had to try coffee for the first time at some point in your life."

"True," Chad agreed and took a sip of his coffee. "Is it too early to get a cup of soup to go?"

"Nope, not at all. It's Broccoli Cheddar or Pepper Jack."

"Pepper Jack sounds good."

Katherine brought him his soup and sandwich. "Will you and Maggie be coming to church Sunday?"

Chad stiffened. "I don't know…Maggie'll probably come with the kids."

"Why don't you come with them? It would be good to see you all together. And I think you would like Pastor Harris."

"I'll think about it…I don't know…I'm just not into all that church stuff." Chad shifted on his stool. He liked coming to Katherine's place, but he didn't like it when she brought up God and church. He was a good enough guy. He didn't need the religion crutch.

Katherine smiled. "Harper is in my Sunday School Class. She asked me last week to pray you would come to church…and she wanted me to invite you to come. I told her she should invite you herself, but she said she didn't think you would listen to her."

Chad looked at Katherine. "Harper said that?" his voice sounded pained as he thought of his nine year old daughter.

"Yes, she did." Katherine was glad Chad was upset. So many fathers didn't seem to care these days.

He shook his head, his cheeks turning pink. "I might just come, if for no other reason than to make Harper happy."

"That would be a good idea. And tell Harper why you came. It'll do her heart good."

"I'll do that...if I come," Chad said, a very big 'if' in his tone. "Well, I gotta get back to my beat. Merry Christmas!"

"Merry Christmas, Chad."

Katherine stood by the front window of her shop, watching as the snow fell to the ground, praying no one got hurt in this storm.

Obviously the police officers had the same idea, for within ten minutes, they had a road block set up. Upon inquiring, Katherine learned the main highway in Bluefield was a mess of car accidents and no one was allowed on it for at least four hours...and that was only if the snow stopped. Otherwise, it would be even longer.

Katherine went back to the kitchen to stir the soup and check the sandwiches. The radio got louder as the daily scripture verse was read. It caught her attention and a smile spread across her face as she reached over to turn it up a little. It was Bryson's favorite verse. *"Be still and know that I am God."*

Bryson had always said that verse made him remember God was in control and even if bad things happened, God was still God. Very reassuring, especially when one was having a rough day on the job.

The music resumed and Katherine's mind wandered back to their first Christmas together as a married couple. They had been stationed in Germany. Their place wasn't big, just a kitchen/living room, bathroom and bedroom. But they hadn't cared.

Their Christmas "feast" hadn't been the norm either...home fried chicken, macaroni and cheese, corn, green beans and biscuits. But Bryson had said just being together made it Christmas. The food didn't matter.

Dessert had made it seem more like a banquet: Katherine's signature Chocolate Chip Trifle, with a touch of coffee flavor. She only had the ingredients for a small one, making it a true, "trifle of this and a trifle of that."

Bryson had teased her all through their marriage that it was tasting her trifle at a servicemen's dinner that had made him want to get to know her better. She would just laugh and say he was crazy.

Katherine smiled at these pleasant memories. She remembered how they had cleaned up the kitchen together, then sat on their small loveseat to read the Christmas story. Katherine had always liked the Luke 2 account of the Nativity. She had a vivid imagination and with Bryson as narrator, the story came alive in her mind's eye.

Afterwards, they had exchanged a few small gifts. She could still see the pleasure in Bryson's hazel eyes at finally getting a new watch. The old one was begging to be thrown away. But the real pleasure had come when he opened the package containing the personalized calendar she had made for him. The smile he gave her was priceless.

She had been equally pleased with the gifts he'd given her: a locket with their wedding pictures inside and a decorative motto that said, "I will Never Leave Thee Nor Forsake Thee."

Katherine fingered the locket around her neck and mentally pictured the motto on her nightstand at home. They were treasured gifts to her.

They had sat together on the sofa and sang snatches of their favorite Christmas songs, never finishing them, just singing their favorite phrases...

The jingling of the bells on the front door jarred her from her reverie.

Chapter 4
The Writer

Hatred stirreth up strifes: but love covereth all sins.
Proverbs 10:12

"Yes, Charlie, I'm stuck in a hick town because of a snowstorm." The tall, slender young woman rolled her eyes at the unheard comments the other party was making. Katherine noticed the blue eyed blonde's fashionable dress and aristocratic air right away...and an undercurrent of intense observation. Already she had taken in all the features of the small shop.

She placed her laptop case, purse and travel bag on a table and sat down, not even glancing in Katherine's direction. "Well, I've been trying to tell you, there's a road block and I'm stranded. Yes, in a little coffee shop...rather quaint actually. Yes, they have free Wi-Fi...Of course I'll meet my deadline! Have you ever known *me* to be late? Yeah, whatever, just have my apartment cleaned on Friday...*Yes*, no later than Saturday! Whatever...Good *bye!*"

She tapped the screen, muttering, "And good riddance!" The twenty something year old took in her surroundings once more. "*Magnifique!*" she breathed. "It's perfect."

Katherine smiled as the young woman approached the counter. "Merry Christmas! What can I get for ya?"

Scanning the menu, the lady replied, "I'll have the Salted Caramel Latté. That has to be my favorite." Under her breath she added, "Even though that's like *so* last year!" She paid for her order, and Katherine gave her the passcode to the internet connection.

"*OH!* Is that a *real* WWII Garrison's Cap?" she exclaimed, hurrying over to the military display.

Katherine smiled. "Yes, it belonged to my grandfather. He was a prisoner of war in Germany from 1944 until the end of the European war."

"No kidding? What branch was he in?"

"Uh...Army Air Corps[1], I believe...I at least know he was in a plane that was shot down. He was about 19 when that happened."

The young woman had a note pad out, jotting down the facts given to her. "Oh, I'm Bella Cunningham, and I write books for the Prose and Polish Literary Firm in New York City. I'm currently working on a WWII project about a POW. Could you give me some more information? I will of course keep your family member's name out of it."

"Oh, sure. He was 17 when he joined the Air Corps. I think he was being flown over France when they were shot down...and he was badly injured when his parachute landed."

Katherine resisted the urge to shutter. "I think Grandma said he broke his leg and at least two ribs, plus scratches and bruises. He got so tangled up in his chute, the Nazis had to cut him loose.

"The Germans tried to get him to march out, but he couldn't walk on his bad leg. One of the soldiers carried him out over his shoulder. When they brought him to the prison

---

[1] Most people refer to the air power of WWII as the US Army Air Corp, when in reality the name was changed to U.S. Army Air Force in 1941. Old habits are hard to break ☺

28

camp, he was locked in a cell for several days. A camp doctor finally saw to him and released him into the camp."

Katherine handed Bella her drink. "I don't know a whole lot about his prison stay, other than that he and some other prisoners attempted an escape and were soundly punished." Again she grimaced, picturing the scar on her grandfather's face from the retribution. "They were liberated in May of 1945."

"Amazing," Bella mumbled, scribbling some cryptic notes on her paper. "Is he still living?"

Katherine nodded. "Yes, but he doesn't like to talk about his time in prison...he told my husband more than he ever told me, but my grandma might share some with you."

"That would be great. Here's my card, if you would be so kind as to pass it on to her."

"I sure will," Katherine replied, placing the card under the counter. "So, how many books have you written?"

Bella smiled, pleased Katherine was interested. "I just released my tenth novel, *New York New Year*, sequel to *City Girl Christmas*. But my ultimate best seller is my debut novel, *The Big Apple Girls*. It's somewhat a comedy, somewhat a mystery."

Katherine nodded. "I believe I've seen *The Big Apple Girls* at the library! I've never read it though. I'll certainly have to check it out."

"Please do! Well, I'd better get to work on my plotting." Bella strolled back to her chair and sat down. It wasn't long before the sound of fingernails on a keyboard trickled from that corner of the room.

Bella wasn't the only one who took in detail. Katherine discovered from looking at Bella's travel bag that the young woman was a traveler, with stickers from Paris, London, Tokyo, Berlin, Rome and Moscow, to name a few.

Her phone rang and she quickly swiped the screen and brought it to her ear. "Bella C., what can I do for you?...The Winter Collection is releasing in three days...Yes, I have two pieces that were accepted, the Winter Blue beret and the Paris

Inspired sweater set...I am working on a piece for the Spring...yeah, something light and fresh, I'm going wild with peach and wisteria...oh, I like! Donna, email those to me and I'll see if it's what we need...I know! I love my second job! I've got the best of both worlds, writing novels and designing clothes. What's next? Hollywood?...Huh! In my dreams. Maybe the Christmas experts will notice my expertise soon..."

Katherine's smile faded as she heard the words. The beautiful fresh-faced girl was headed for a big disappointment. From the sounds of it, she was quite talented, but knowing how the world is, Katherine knew they would chew Bella up and spit her out when they were done with her. Katherine's heart went out to the girl.

"...Nah, I don't think I'm spreading myself too thin. I've got everything under control...right. Talk to you tomorrow then. Bye." Bella returned to her typing, humming to herself.

Waiting until Bella didn't look so occupied, Katherine asked, "So, are you trying to get home for Christmas?"

"Home?" Bella repeated. "Nah, I'm going to my best friend's house to spend Christmas with her family. Then I'll head back to New York."

"Does your family live in New York?" Katherine inquired, drying a glass as she spoke.

Bella got a far off look in her eyes. "My family...no, they don't. I haven't seen them since I was little...you know, my parents died in a car accident and I was raised by my aunt, but she's not a 'family bonds' kind of person. I'm fine on my own. I can take care of myself."

"I see," Katherine replied, half amused, half disturbed. "I'm sorry about your parents. I'm fortunate to live near some of my family. I'm one of those people that have to be around others."

Bella managed a small hint of a smile. "Well, I won't be alone forever. I'll be getting married soon...we'll see how that goes." She turned back to her manuscript and Katherine took that as the "end of conversation" cue.

But she was mistaken. Bella studied her carefully before asking, "Do you like living in a small town like this?"

Katherine laughed. "Oh, it's not all that small. It just has the small town values and traditions. But yes, I like the slow pace. I love the people here and I like to think they love having me here. I'm originally from Texas, and this was my husband's home town. I loved it before I came here, because he loved it so much."

"How did you two meet, him living here in North Carolina?" Bella asked, arching her brow.

Katherine leaned against the counter. "We met in church. I was the church organist, and he was a soldier just out of boot camp, stationed at Ft. Hood. He came to our church his first Sunday in town with a friend of his. They were both good, Godly young men from Christian families. That's not something we ran across often in our area.

"Bryson joined our church and when he could, he participated in church ministries and activities, as did his friend, Dan. Dan was from here too, but he visited as often as he could. He and Bryson were pretty close." Katherine's face burst into a smile. "Bryson and I married four years later, right before he was stationed in Germany. Dan married my sister Isabelle two years after us."

Katherine almost forgot Bella was there. "I certainly didn't plan to marry a serviceman. I love our military, but I never believed that would be my 'calling,' so to speak. And believe me, it is a calling. I imagined myself living a storybook life, living in my home town with my husband, probably a rancher. Instead, God let me marry a soldier and move all over the place. I learned sleepless nights worrying over his safety were better spent in prayer. After all, worry wouldn't help him any when he was deployed, but prayer would."

Bella stirred her latté. "You talk like you really believe God controls everything, marriage, safety…like somehow, He's got the right to plan your life!"

Katherine looked at Bella and couldn't help a gentle laugh. "Well, He created everything and allowed us to exist.

Don't you think He has the right to plan the life of His creations? Who are we to tell Him no?"

Bella stared at Katherine. "You're serious! Wow…I've never met a fanatic before!"

Now Katherine really laughed. "Well, now you have! Would you like an autograph?"

Bella's face flushed slightly, and she couldn't help but join Katherine in her amusement. "That was rather brusque of me. I'm sorry. But I've never met anyone who really believed God had those kind of rights…even so called Christians…" She shook her head. "Anyway, have you ever wanted to move anywhere else?"

Katherine accepted Bella's change of topics with a smile. "Sometimes. I like visiting family and a few close friends, but somehow, this is home. I can't seem to break away from it. What about you?"

"Give me Paris!" She leaned back in her chair, a dreamy look in her eyes. "I love that place! If I could live there, I would be *so* happy!"

"I'm sure it's a beautiful place," Katherine replied.

"Beautiful…there are no words to describe it! The shops, the food, the history, the culture…ahhh! When it was bombed last year, I thought I'd die!"

"That was a shame-"

Their conversation was interrupted by the door opening, bringing with it a blast of cold air, swirling snowflakes and Deputy Kyle Pickett. "Afternoon, Mrs. Shannon. Could I get a cappuccino –I mean a V-day Special– to-go? I just found out I'm finally getting an upgrade on my squad car!"

"That's certainly worth celebrating! How's your family doing, Deputy?"

"Missing you!" the middle-aged man replied. "They're finally getting over that stomach bug. They're looking forward to the 'Post-Christmas Play' next weekend."

Katherine handed him his drink. "I'm glad to hear they're doing better. Tell them all I said hello and I miss them too."

"Will do. Oh, I forgot," Kyle reached into his pocket and pulled out a coloring page. "Andy colored that for you."

"The little sweetheart! Stop by here when you get off shift and I'll send some soup home with you for the little ones."

"Thank you! I'll do that." Kyle glanced at his watch. "I gotta go. See ya' at church. Merry Christmas!"

"Merry Christmas!" Katherine replied.

Kyle turned to leave. Bella watched him with a jaded stare. "Merry Christmas," he said to her as he headed for the door.

Bella glared at him and turned back to her manuscript, refusing to return the polite greeting. She jostled her travel bag, catching the Policeman's attention. One look at her stickers and he knew what the problem was. Kyle glanced back at Katherine, then shrugged it off and left the store.

Katherine pressed her lips in a thin line as she looked at Bella. What had Kyle seen? He'd been both surprised and hurt by whatever it was. Making up her mind, Katherine went to the table behind Bella's table to see what had disturbed Kyle.

That's when she saw the two stickers. One said in bold red letters, "Police Brutality is Terrorism." The second depicted a police officer standing with his arms crossed. The slogan declared, "The American Terrorist."

Katherine's eyes flashed as she turned back to the counter. She flicked her dish towel in an irritated manner. Should she say anything to Bella about her behavior, and those ridiculous stickers?

Instead, she began "cleaning" the police display on the opposite wall, making noise that couldn't be ignored. Bella glanced up in annoyance. A canvas art piece caught her attention. It was black with a thin blue stripe on it. In white lettering it said, "If you don't support our Police Force, Don't bother calling 9-1-1!"

Bella stared at Katherine, a peculiar look on her face. Their eyes met. Katherine refused to break the stare, trying to read Bella's expression. Bella decided mentally not to make any further demonstrations. What went over just fine in New York City obviously wasn't accepted in North Carolina, at least not at Katherine's place.

In spite of their disagreement over the policemen, Bella knew a good story when she saw one. And all that mattered to her was the perfect story, whether she personally liked it or not. She took notes about Katherine, her appearance, mannerisms, some things she had said. Then she jotted down a brisk description of Deputy Pickett. Next, the interior of the shop...yeah, this would be an awesome setting for a novel.

She had just started some structure plotting when the sound of the bells met her ears. At first, she ignored it, thinking it was possibly another police officer. She wasn't snubbing this time...she was busy. She wouldn't even-

The unmistakable sound of metal scraping the floor met her trained ear. Her curiosity got the better of her. She glanced back, her eyes instantly filling with the sight of a metal leg brace.

Chapter 5
Wounded Spirit

He healeth the broken in heart, and bindeth up their wounds.
Psalm 147:3

He was young, younger than Bella. Probably barely into his twenties, at least by appearance. He wore a police uniform with CPL. ERICSON on one side of his shirt. His dark hair was short, his eyes held a look of weariness.

The brace was strapped around his right knee, ending under the sole of his shoe. As he stepped toward the counter, he grimaced. He had to stop for a moment, gripping the back of a chair for support. Bella watched him with curiosity, her malice for his profession momentarily forgotten. What had happened to him?

Then recognition filled her eyes. She set her jaw and jerked her head away. She hoped he wouldn't say anything to her. She had *plenty* she wanted to say to him.

The young man limped up to the counter. Katherine smiled warmly at the policeman. "Merry Christmas! What can I get for ya?"

He grunted a low greeting, then glanced at the menu. Something in his eyes lit up. "What's 'The Squad Car Special?"

Katherine's contagious laughter was her first response. "It's coffee and your choice of a pastry. The nickname makes it more interesting. It's sort of a joke between me and a friend."

A hint of a smile played at his lips. "Sounds good to me. I'll take a Squad Car Special, Ma'am. A Blueberry Danish will be fine."

"Coming right up." He reached for his wallet and Katherine put up her hand. "The first one is always on the house to say thank you for your service."

He looked up at her, questions in his eyes. "Oh...thanks, Ms...."

"Shannon, Katherine Shannon," she replied.

"Thanks, Ms. Shannon. I'm Justin Ericson."

Katherine shook hands with him. "Thank you so much for your service."

He nodded. "Thank you for your support."

Katherine handed him his order and watched as he limped over to a corner booth. She shook her head as he stared out the window.

Justin took a sip of coffee, trying to shut out pictures dancing through his head: signs held by angry protesters...people with knives, guns and nasty words on their lips...and the poor confused citizens trying to figure out which way was the safest way to run...

Bella dropped her cell phone, sending a loud *boom* echoing through the small shop. Justin jumped as the noise jarred him from his thoughts. For a moment, he had forgotten he was away from the fuss and bother. Safe.

He closed his eyes. *That was bright, Ericson,* he chided. *It's just a stupid cell phone!*

Justin looked up as Katherine neared his vicinity with her dust cloth and cleaning spray. She set to work cleaning a display on the wall near him.

He glanced up at her, then looked down, staring into his cup. He looked back up at her. Katherine noticed. Was this a movement of nervousness or an invitation to a conversation?

36

She took a chance on the latter being correct. "Are you from nearby?"

Justin acted surprised that she was speaking to him. "Next town over...My family lives in South Carolina. I'm going to my brother's for Christmas, and he lives about two hours from here."

"Oh, how nice! You don't hear of many brothers getting together for Christmas. Is he married?"

"Yeah...Cindy's her name. Nice girl."

Katherine smiled. "That's good. It's nice to have good in-laws. Do they have children?"

Justin glanced out the window real quick before replying. "They have three kids. Two girls and a boy," he added, thinking she would like the details.

"Oh, what are their names? How old are they?"

"Allie's five, Clare's two and Nick's...oh...about four months old I think."

"Oh, how sweet! When's the last time you saw them?" Katherine asked, wiping dust off a motto.

Justin rolled his eyes back as he tried to add up the time. He wiped his hand across his brow. "About ten months I guess. Haven't met Nick yet."

"That's a long time!"

He shrugged. "I keep pretty busy." He jerked his head to stare out the frosted window once more. He winced and rubbed his leg.

"Is your leg alright?"

"It's fine, just bruised up. I was able to convince the doctors this morning to release me to drive. Bad enough to keep me off work for a while, though. That's why I'm trying to get to my house to pack and go to South Carolina." The explanation sounded forced, like he was trying to make up a convincing story.

"I'm sorry," Katherine said softly. Justin squirmed under her sincere gaze.

Desperate to keep from answering more questions, Justin glanced at the Vintage style Police display. "The guy in the photo-frame, who's he?"

Katherine didn't even have to look back to answer. "My husband, Bryson. He joined the Police Force after he got out of the Army. He was a combat medic."

Justin looked up quickly. "Why did he join the Police? Why not EMS?"

"That's what I asked him when he first told me," Katherine said with a hint of a laugh in her voice. "He told me it was always good to have a man on the team who knew medicine. And with his experience in the military, it seemed the most logical thing for him to do. At least that's what he said."

He stared back down at his coffee cup. Bella squirmed in her chair. No wonder Mrs. Shannon was so protective of the Policemen. Her husband was one of them!

"So, are you going to make a full recovery?" Katherine asked.

Back to me again, Justin thought. *She's clever.* "Yeah, I have to wear the brace until February. I'll be fine after that."

Her face lit up with a beautiful smile. "That's wonderful! I hope your recovery is a fast process. Thank you for being willing to go out there. This country would certainly be in a mess if our policemen weren't doing their job. We take you boys for granted too often."

Red flushed across Justin's face at her words. "Thank you for saying so. Sometimes it does feel like no one remembers we're out there…they forget we're people!"

Katherine nodded in agreement. "To read the news, you'd think so. But there are still some of us who remember you fellows are indeed humans, who just happen to have a very stressful and important job. What made you want to be a policeman?"

Justin took another sip of his coffee. "I was six when 9/11 took place, but I remember it distinctly. I was sitting in the living room with my mom; she was reading to me. Dad

38

called from work and told her to turn on the news. I thought it was a scary movie. I didn't know until I was a little older that all that was real. How do you explain a terrorist attack to a six year old?

"Anyway, my uncle was a policeman and he told us about all the men who risked their lives to protect the American home front. Sounded real noble, important. So I decided that's what I wanted to do. He didn't tell me it was a thankless job most of the time, but then, I didn't join up to get thanked."

Katherine shivered. "I was working in the kitchen when 9/11 happened. My husband was actually out on training when I got the news. He called me and told me what had happened. I was in too much shock to comprehend what it all meant...until he told me he would be getting active duty orders soon. That's when it all hit me. And when he left, I was so afraid I'd never see him again."

Glancing at Bella, Katherine noticed she had been listening to at least the last bit of their conversation. "How about you, Miss Cunningham? Where were you when 9/11 happened?"

Bella twirled a strand of blonde hair around her finger as she replied, "I was at school. I remember we had an emergency drill that day...and all the teachers were all choked up. And that's the only time I ever heard the principal pray over the loud speaker. After that, we had state of emergency drills for a solid week, then once every other week for at least two months."

"That's sad you'd never heard prayer in school before then!" Katherine shook her head. "God has been so merciful to our country by keeping the fighting overseas."

They sat in silence for a moment. How could the fighting have lasted this long? Fifteen long years...

Katherine turned back to Justin. "So, do you go to church anywhere?"

Justin shrugged. "Sometimes. I used to go with my sergeant once in a while. He always goes and tries to get me to go all the time too, but it just wasn't for me."

"Oh, church is for everyone," Katherine replied pleasantly. "So where does he attend church?"

Justin's lips pressed together in a thin line. He shook his head to clear his thoughts. "Can't remember the name, but he says he's an 'Independent, Fundamental Baptist.' He has a long string of other stuff he said with it, but I don't remember it all. Something about the kind of Bible he reads is in there somewhere."

"King James Only? Is that what he says?" Katherine inquired.

Justin nodded in affirmation. "That's it."

Katherine smiled. "That's my beliefs as well."

"Thought you might be," he said, his voice low. He glanced around. "I'll have to tell him about this place when he gets out of the hospital." He regretted the words when he saw Bella look at him.

Katherine stopped dusting. "Your sergeant's in the hospital? Wait, were you both involved with that riot the other day?"

Justin nodded slowly. "Yep. Word gets around doesn't it?"

"My brother-in-law was telling me about it. I'm glad you are both alright! What about the sergeant's family?" Katherine asked. "How are they doing?"

Justin exhaled. "They're doing okay."

"Will he be home in time for Christmas?"

"No. But his wife's bringing the kids over so they can be together."

Katherine's heart went out to the kids. Christmas was to be spent at home, not in a hospital.

Bella's nose twitched. "Uh…Mrs. Shannon, do you smell something?"

Katherine snapped out of her thoughts as Justin remarked, "Smells like something burning."

Chapter 6
Career Girl

Every good gift and every perfect gift is from above, and cometh down from the Father of lights, with whom is no variableness, neither shadow of turning.
James 1:17

"It's just the cookies," she announced racing to another oven in the kitchen. "Thank the Lord, I don't think they're burned..." She pulled the pan out of the oven and placed them on the counter.

Bella offered a smile, though she wasn't sure if she would order a cookie at lunch time. Justin drank the last of his coffee. He personally liked his cookies a little dark.

Katherine placed the cookies on a platter, becoming a little less sure these cookies would be sellable. She glanced sheepishly over at Bella. "I think I'll just put on another batch."

"I think I would," Bella agreed.

Katherine took down some cookie dough she'd frozen earlier and laid it out to thaw.

"Are you gonna throw those out?" Justin called.

Katherine looked at him uncertainly. "Who would eat them?"

"I would."

Katherine shrugged. "If you want them, you can have them."

Justin nodded with a slight smile. "I'll just take a couple for now."

Katherine placed two on a napkin and took them over to Justin. "You really *like* 'well-done' cookies?" she asked, still not believing it.

"Yes, ma'am."

"Why?"

Justin shrugged. "They kinda grew on me after a trick was pulled on me as a rookie. I brought a baggie of cookies with my lunch everyday. Before long the boys started swapping them on me...with burnt cookies."

"Oh, no!" Katherine exclaimed.

Justin half smiled. "I didn't care. A cookie's a cookie. So the joke ended up being on them."

The door swung open and slammed shut. "Yeah, completely blocked off, Dad," a loud voice announced. Justin jerked his head to look at the intruder.

The brown headed green-eyed girl continued talking loudly into her phone. "Yes, I'll be home as soon as I can. I'm just gonna hang out at Mrs. Shannon's coffee shop until it clears up. Sgt. Piper said it'll be a few hours...okay. Love you too. Bye."

She looked up at Katherine and hurried over to give her a hug. "Hi, Mrs. Shannon! Messy weather huh?"

Katherine laughed and hugged the college kid back. "At least it's a *pretty* mess. How are things at the Hannover place, Nicole?"

Nicole flashed a bright smile at her church friend. "The family's doing great. I was on my way home from shopping and nearly slid into the street lamp!"

"Oh, Cole!" Katherine gasped. "Are you alright?"

Musical laughter left the girl's lips. "I'm absolutely fine, Mrs. Shannon. Sgt. Piper helped me get the car back on the road and off the sidewalk. There was some ice...and speeding wasn't a factor," she added quickly, noticing Justin sitting there.

Nicole plopped her book bag down on a nearby table. "Can I get a mocha? I'm *soooo* cold!"

"Of course you can," Katherine replied, giving Nicole change for the $5.00 bill she had given her.

Glancing down at her phone, Nicole squealed, "I missed a call from Amber! How could I miss a call from my bestie? Oh!" She hit redial and pressed the phone against her ear as she carried her drink back to her table. "Hello, Amber? Nicole! Yeah! I'm *soooo* sorry I missed your call...yeah I was on the phone with my dad. The snow's left me stranded at Mrs. Shannon's...not a bad place to get stuck, right?...Yeah, I'm just glad I had my study bag with me...uh-huh...really? That's *forte*, Amber! I know, I love Christmas too! I think I'm gonna finally get that music writing program I told you about...yeah the updated one...really? Cool! Where did you see that? Just out, huh? What's it called? Okay..." Nicole scribbled a line on her notebook.

"What? Oh!" she burst into hysterical laughter. Bella cut her eyes over at the newcomer and glowered. She pulled her earbuds from her bag and jammed them into the jack on her laptop.

"...The scholarship is like my dream come true, Amber! I'll have a chance at being a concert pianist! I think I'm gonna accept..."

"...Yes, Jonathan and Becky are getting married in August...Yeah, I'll be here for it, and I wouldn't be leaving until September...I know, it's so *forte*!"

Justin crossed his arms and sighed heavily. Who cared if she had a chance for a full music scholarship to study abroad? And that phrase she kept saying, "That's *forte*!" What was it supposed to mean?

Katherine sat behind the counter, her head propped on the palm of her hand. When would Nicole ever be off the phone? Couldn't she at least quieten down?

"...Sarah told Mom this morning baby number 3 is on the way! Yeah! I can't wait!"

"...Well, I'd better let you go...okay, see ya' later!"

Justin gave an involuntary sigh of relief. Bella took her earbuds out, hoping to make a point. Nicole seemed oblivious to their disturbance. She pulled out a folder, making hurried strokes with her pencil across the assignment pages.

Katherine glanced up at the clock. "If y'all are hungry, I have some soup ready. And since y'all are kinda stranded here, it's on the house."

"I'll take some," Nicole said. "Your soup's the best!"

Bella glanced toward the counter. "What kind of soup is it?"

Katherine replied, "Broccoli Cheddar Soup or Broccoli Pepper Jack Soup, whichever you prefer."

"The Cheddar sounds good, thank you."

"I'll go with Pepper Jack," Justin decided.

"Coming right up."

The girls moved up to the counter, but Justin remained in his corner booth in his seclusion. Katherine served the soup and sandwiches and glasses of water.

Katherine took her seat and reached for *The Day She Fell*, hoping she could get to a happier note in the story.

Nicole glanced at the name tag clipped to the bottom of Bella's stylish cream colored shirt. "You're *Bella Cunningham*?" she gasped.

Katherine looked up as the question was asked. Bella looked at Nicole incredulously. "Yes, I am. You've heard of me, I assume?"

"Have I ever! Oh, this is *forte*! I *love* your books! That's why my friend was trying to call me, to let me know your newest book was out! Oh! I have *Simone* with me! Could you sign it?"

Bella straightened and smiled, forgetting how annoyed she had been with Nicole earlier. "Of course I will."

The book was placed on the counter and signed by the flattered author. "My favorites were your French Résistance

Series! Madeline was amazing. I cried like through the whole story!"

Katherine closed her book to see the cover. Why hadn't she seen it before? There was the author's name in swirly type: Bella Cunningham.

"I wish I could have you sign this one, Bella," she called. "But it belongs to the library. You are a truly compelling writer. Madeline is a well thought out person. She seems so real...too real sometimes."

Bella smiled a genuinely pleased smile. "Thank you so much for saying so. I had the hardest edits on that series, trying to pull people in. I'm thinking on trying my hand at a series on the German Resistance group, The White Rose."

"Please do!" Nicole begged, "It would be *so* neat!"

The girls continued to talk, moving to another table so they could talk more one on one. Katherine's eyes were glued to the page she was reading.

"Silence, that riveting thing that can nearly paralyze one with fear and uncertainty. Madeline willed herself forward. She had to look out the window to make sure Karle had escaped. Footsteps pounded outside her door and shouts in that tongue she had come to hate added to the noise. Why did her hands feel so heavy?

At last she was able to manipulate her hands into reaching out to pull back the curtain just a touch. Inches away, the German soldiers bickered back and forth. But Karle was nowhere in sight.

*"It **is** your fault," one of the soldiers spat in his comrade's face. "You are the one who missed the shot. Now we will have no end of trouble from him! He is still at large to sabotage our operations here in Paris! And we don't even have a clue what he looks like!" His voice was more like a screech than a shout. Madeline smiled. Karle was safe.*

Katherine hadn't known she was holding her breath until she released it. Madeline's brother-in-law had escaped. After all, he was only sixteen, and such a vital part of the Résistance.

She glanced over at Justin, who was scraping the last bit of soup from his bowl. "Would you like some more?" she asked him. He didn't reply. "Sir?"

Justin looked up, startled out of his thoughts. "Ma'am?" Katherine repeated her offer. "Uh, sure if it's not much trouble."

Katherine smiled. "None at all." She ladled the thick soup into his bowl and returned it to his table. Katherine returned to her book, eager to find out what the Résistance team would be up to next.

Justin ate his soup in silence, watching the snow fall. He'd once heard every snowflake was uniquely different. Sgt. Baker had told him so the morning of the riot. They had been wishing for a good dose of snow. Sgt. Baker had told him God was so creative, He could come up with a different pattern for every snowflake that ever was.

Justin sighed and ate some more soup. A lot of good all that talk had done. He and the sergeant had more important things on their minds now. Like trying to hang onto their jobs...

"So you have a website?" he heard Nicole ask Bella.

Bella nodded. "Yes, I'll give you my business card. The information is on there. My email is too, so you could email me about those WWII songs you were talking about."

"Sure, I'd love to! Now, tell me, what was your inspiration for *What's in Your Purse?*"

"Well, I was actually cleaning out my purse one day and I got to thinking about how all that junk got there. Then I thought about what other people may carry with them and then, Addison Parley introduced herself to my stash of character names..."

Justin rolled his eyes. *Such nonsense,* he thought. His brow furrowed. Where had he seen that blonde before? She looked so familiar.

Nicole shook her head in amazement. "I wish I could get that creative on my music compositions for school!"

"I'm sure you've got one you're proud of," Bella urged.

Nicole thought for a moment. "Yes...I do like a piece I did last year, *When the Wild Geese Call.*' Funny name, but that's what it made me think of. All I could picture was a lake surrounded by autumn trees and wild geese migrating."

"Sounds enchanting! I wish I could hear it," Bella lamented.

Nicole's eyes lit up. "I have it recorded on my phone! Hang on..." She pulled out her device and began swiping and tapping, searching for her recording.

At last it was found and the instrumental music filled that corner of the shop. It was pretty, a beautiful blending of classical and folk elements. Bella listened intently, wheels of inspiration turning in her brain. Nicole could tell she liked it.

In his corner booth, Justin closed his eyes, relaxing to the soothing sound of the piano. He'd always taken a fancy to good music.

Katherine missed the music; she was reading *The Day She Fell* again.

Madeline ran her fingers across the water in the fountain, watching the ripples that bubbled and bounced from her touch. A few leaves swirled through the air as she turned to face the young soldier.

"Pvt. Hoffer, I do hope you may one day return to your family. You are too young to lose everything you know. Too innocent. Oh! May you keep that innocence! Were this war not invading every aspect of our lives, I believe you and my brother would have made good friends."

The ruddy cheeked boy cocked his head to study the older woman. She made him think of his oldest sister. "I wish Paris were beautiful," he said looking around. Many structures had been mended, but the scars of the attack still hinted it had once been a glorious, magnificent place.

"I wish it were too, Private." She turned to look him full in the face. "Don't let your officers and companions turn you into the kind of person who would do a thing like this. Don't become a rogue. Be different."

She swept her hand, indicating the town. *"When you are tempted to do some cruel act of violence, remember Paris. Remember the people who were hurt by her destruction. Remember what you told me about your hometown."*

The boy averted his eyes, following an orange leaf as it slipped into a gutter. He wanted to forget about his neighbors at home that had been rounded up and forced to leave...Jacob, Yoshi and David. They were all gone...where were they now?

He looked back at Madeline. *"I will never be like them. I want something different for myself."* He glanced around, then lowered his voice. *"I won't tell them about the American pilot you are hiding in the crypt."*

Madeline looked at him sharply. How had he known?

Katherine was pulled from the story by the sound of shoes stomping on the small porch of her shop. She looked up and smiled. The lunch rush was about to start.

Chapter 7
Deep Wounds

For we have not an high priest which cannot be touched with the feeling of our infirmities; but was in all points tempted like as we are, yet without sin.
Hebrews 4:15

Sgt. Piper was the first in the door. "I hope you've got something good and warm on the stove, Mrs. Shannon," he teased his sister-in-law, "Because we're chilled to the bone!" He took off his hat and sat at his favorite stool at the counter.

"I thought you boys would be burning up out there," Katherine said with a laugh. "Sure you don't want me to turn on the A/C?"

Laughter rippled across the group of four officers that had entered the shop. Katherine took their orders and headed to the back to get their food.

After serving the men and waiting for Dan to finish blessing his food, Katherine whispered, "Dan, see that young man in the back corner?"

Dan nonchalantly glanced over his shoulder. "I see him. What about him?"

"Don't you recognize him?"

Dan narrowed his eyes. "Not sure."

"Well, you should. You were just telling me about him this morning!"

Dan's head swiveled back to look at Justin. "Oh! Yes, now I recognize him."

Katherine told Dan about her conversation with him. "He's pretty upset about what happened to his sergeant. Could you maybe talk to him?"

"I can give it a try," Dan decided. "Pray for me."

Katherine nodded. Silently, she prayed for Dan as he crossed the room. *Lord, help him reach Justin for You! Draw Justin to the Help he needs the most!*

"Howdy," Dan said, standing next to Justin's booth. "Mind if I join you?"

Justin jerked his head up. His face flushed. "Sure...I guess," he stammered.

Dan sat across from him. "Sgt. Dan Piper."

"Cpl. Justin Ericson. I saw you at the hospital this morning. Thank you for coming out to check on Sgt. Baker."

The two shook hands. "Think nothing of it, just checking on a brother."

Justin shrugged. "I guess you're right."

Dan nodded. "How's your leg?"

"It'll be fine. That's the least of my worries though."

"I think you and –was it Sgt. Tyler Baker?– have a solid case in your favor. Everyone could see you were within your rights to fire. I'll be praying everything gets sorted out."

Justin emitted a slight, humorless laugh. "We'll see how much good praying does." He gazed out the window, then down at his bowl of half eaten soup.

Dan arched an eyebrow. "You think it won't?"

Justin looked up at him and said, "Not really."

"Why not?" Dan asked.

Justin shook his head. "Doesn't matter."

"Sure it does," Dan said.

Justin's eyes snapped and his jawline tightened. "God didn't help us when we asked Him to! He didn't-" Justin's voice cracked and he stopped.

"What are you talking about?" Dan asked. His voice didn't indicate a request for information; it was more like a demand.

Justin took a deep breath and let it out slowly. "At the riot the other day, we were standing them off. The crowd was getting tense and Sgt. Baker was trying to keep everybody calm." He paused, trying to bring himself to continue. Sweat stood out on the young man's forehead.

"Sgt. Baker, prayed...prayed God would watch over us and help us get back safely; that no one would be hurt...He believed God would do it too. And...and I was convinced everything would turn out right."

Justin closed his eyes and licked his lips. Dan waited for him to continue. As he told the story, Justin felt he was reliving it...

A brick sailed through the air, smashing into Justin's knee. No one knew who had thrown it. Justin was lying on the ground; no matter how hard he tried, he couldn't stand. Tyler was kneeling over him, shielding him. Justin watched as two of the rioters edged closer to the perimeter made by the police.

Justin was surprised to see a sophisticated looking young woman in the group, shouting slogans along with everyone else. She looked down at Justin, a sinister smile removing any beauty she might have possessed. She was snapping pictures on her phone.

Police sirens were blaring; reinforcements had arrived. Everything would be alright. Tyler helped Justin sit up. That's when the riot really broke out. Pushing, shoving, fists swinging...and the shouting. Tyler tried to get Justin out of there.

A rioter ran at them, his gun pointed at Justin. But Tyler took the bullet, pushing Justin to safety. He hit the ground again, scraping his shoulder. The rioter cocked his gun, intending to shoot the sergeant again.

And that was when Justin fired back.

There was shouting and Justin fell back against the pavement. Gunfire rang in his ears, leaving him temporarily deaf. He fought to keep his eyes open.

"Ericson, are you alright?" But he could barely hear his captain's voice.

"He's gonna be okay," someone else said. "Baker's down."

Those words hit him like an iron fist.

"No!" he had shouted in agony...

Justin rested his head in his hand and closed his eyes.

"It's alright."

Justin looked up. He wasn't at the riot scene. He was in a coffee shop talking to a fellow policeman. Justin turned toward the other side of the shop. His eyes locked on Bella. He set his jaw. Her!

Dan leaned forward, getting Justin's attention. "Is Sgt. Baker saved, Justin?"

Justin clenched his jaw even tighter. "You mean is he a *Christian*? I know all that lingo, Sgt. Piper. Yes, he is a 'born-again' Christian. He tries to get me to be one too and I had seriously been considering it. But when God ignored his prayers, I gave up on it. I can't trust Someone who leaves when you need Him the most!"

"You've got to understand..." Dan started.

Justin cut him off. "I can't!" His body trembled and his knuckles whitened. "Maybe He does nice things for you, but for me, He just keeps taking. Is your mother still living, Sgt. Piper?"

Dan nodded. Justin continued, "Well, mine isn't! He let my mother die a terrible death right after I graduated from the academy! My dad is just wrapped up in his work. Only one of my siblings even seems to recognize that I still exist! I finally have one person I can turn to, somebody I can trust and what happens to him? He gets shot in a riot while asking God to keep us safe. I can't turn my life over to a God that doesn't care!"

52

Dan let him finish his rant. Thankfully, the others in the shop where so absorbed in their own conversations they didn't hear all that was said. He looked into Justin's dark eyes. He was more than angry...he was a soul hurting deeply. He didn't understand the Love of God. Dan was determined to share it with him.

"Greater love hath no man than this, that a man lay down his life for his friends," Dan quoted, his voice low.

Justin's eyebrows bunched. "What?"

"That's the greatest kind of love, laying down your life for someone. That's a principle that's pushed here on the police force." Justin nodded in agreement as Dan continued, "We all have a special bond, like brothers. We can't stand by and let someone 'pick on' our brothers. We've got to stand up for them, even die for them. It's like a natural reaction."

Justin thought of Sgt. Baker. He had purposefully placed himself in harm's way to save Justin's life. He was in the hospital now, because of Justin. And the sergeant would have given his life for him. The weight of that horrid burden saddled itself on Justin.

"Did you know Sgt. Baker wasn't the first man to offer his life for you?" Dan asked.

Justin scowled. "I suppose you're gonna tell me God did too?"

"Sgt. Baker was a good witness, I see," Dan said with a smile.

"It means more when a *brother* offers his life for you," Justin said, looking down.

"Jesus wants to be your Brother. Why else do you think He *died* for you?"

Justin's head shot back up. "Excuse me?"

Dan smiled. He had Justin's attention. He pulled out his pocket New Testament and thumbed through the pages. "The Bible says in Galatians 4:4-7, 'But when the fulness of the time was come, God sent forth his Son, made of a woman, made under the law, To redeem them that were under the law, that we might receive the adoption of sons. And because ye are sons, God hath sent forth the Spirit of his Son into your hearts, crying, Abba, Father. Wherefore thou art no more a servant, but a son; and if a son, then an heir of God through Christ.'

"This is talking about the virgin birth of Christ," Dan explained and Justin nodded. "Jesus was sent to save us from our sins through His death, burial and resurrection. But do you know why He did that?"

Justin raised his eyebrows and Dan continued. "It's because He wanted us to be His 'brothers'. Those verses talk about Salvation being an adoption. And if God is our Father, that makes Jesus our Brother.

"Sgt. Baker offered to give his life for you because you were his 'brother' and he cared about you. He didn't want to see any harm come to you. Likewise, Jesus gave His life for you because He cared for you. He loved you and wanted you to be His brother one day. He didn't want you to spend eternity in hell. So He was willing to die for you to give you that chance."

Justin had never thought of Jesus as a Brother before. "Is that why you hear about people dying for Jesus? Because He's their Brother?"

Dan nodded eagerly. "Yes, you've got it! Those who die for the cause of the Gospel are doing it out of love for their Brother, Jesus Christ. They are called martyrs."

"But if He loves us so much, why didn't He listen to Sgt. Baker when he prayed for God to keep us safe?"

Dan nodded. "That's a good question, Justin. Let me ask you something. Did your mother love you?"

Justin blinked and turned toward the window. "Yeah."

"Did she always give you everything you wanted?"

"No..." Justin said, starting to see where Dan was going with this. He turned back to face Dan.

"Did she stop loving you or quit being your mom just because she said no?"

Justin shook his head.

"Likewise, God doesn't always say yes to our prayers. Sometimes He says 'no' or 'wait'. I can't answer why He chose to let Sgt. Baker get hurt, but I know He had a good reason, though we can't see it. Sometimes on the force, I have to give my men orders that don't make sense to them."

"Sounds familiar," Justin grunted.

Dan laughed. "So, when your superiors give you a strange order and you obey, do they always make sense then?"

"Not always...sometimes it can be several weeks before they make sense in the big picture. Sometimes, I never figure it out." He rubbed the back of his neck. "You're gonna say God's like my officers, aren't you?"

"You catch on pretty quick. Do your officers owe you an explanation?"

Justin gave a half smile. "Officers don't owe a corporal anything. So God, being God, doesn't have to check with us before doing what He wants or telling us what He wants us to do, right?"

"Right."

Justin nodded slowly. The anger had dissipated from his eyes. "I guess Christians always understand what God's doing," he sighed.

Dan shook his head. "Not always, Justin. I had a good friend, Deputy Lewis Gentry, die in my arms during a shootout in my early years in the police force. I can't explain how much it hurt. And like Sgt. Baker, he was shielding me. It was a dark time for me. I couldn't see what God was trying to do. I blamed myself for his death.

"I felt like God had forgotten about me. But God placed another policeman in my path who helped me more than he ever knew. He told me basically what I've been telling you."

Dan paused. He hadn't shared this story in years and the memories stung deeply. He swallowed and continued, motioning to the picture of Bryson hanging on the wall. "That's the policeman, Bryson Shannon. We had been like brothers to each other, and actually married sisters. I don't know if you know this, but Bryson died a year ago today."

Justin glanced at Katherine in surprise, then back to Dan. "No, Mrs. Shannon didn't say anything about that."

55

Dan looked down. "There was an armed robbery at a convenience store. Bryson was called out on the case and got in a high speed chase. He never liked that sort of thing, but he knew what he had to do." Dan sighed. "As they were going around a curve, a suspect shot out one of Bryson's front tires. He lost control of the car and wrapped it around a tree."

Justin shook his head.

Dan continued. "His partner was able to call for help before collapsing. He lived. He and Bryson were rushed to the hospital. They lost Bryson twice in the ambulance. I picked up my wife and his wife, Mrs. Shannon, and headed for the hospital.

"Katherine got in the room just in time to hold his hand before he died. She didn't get to tell him goodbye, that she loved him, anything. But he did squeeze her hand. He knew she was there."

"She seems so happy," Justin said softly.

Dan nodded. "She is, because God is her Savior, and He is always there for her. Ever since Bryson died, us guys on the police force have kinda adopted her as our responsibility. We look after her the best we can, being here when she opens up, taking care of her car maintenance, making sure she gets plenty of business," he said with a laugh. "But she takes care of us too. Any time the scanner goes off, she stops whatever she's doing and prays for us. She prays for our families and anything going on in our lives. You won't find a better prayer warrior."

"Then why did God take her husband from her, if she's such a faithful Christian?" Justin challenged.

"So far, we can't see God's reason for taking Bryson from us. But we do know this: God is always good and God is always right. We have to trust Him."

"It would be easier to trust Him if He felt what we feel. But He can't know how much it hurts," Justin mumbled.

Dan smiled. "How much about the Bible do you know, Justin?"

The young policeman shrugged. "Noah's Ark, the Christmas Story, and Jonah…that's about it."

"Well, the Christmas story is the framework for what's called the New Testament, or the last half of the Bible. When Jesus was born, He was God in the flesh. He lived a perfect life without sin, but He wasn't exempt from heartaches. He had a good friend named Lazarus. Lazarus and his two sisters, Martha and Mary, lived in a place called Bethany and the Bible tells us they were special to Jesus.

"When Lazarus became ill, they sent for Him, knowing He not only would be concerned about His friend but He had the power to heal Lazarus. But Jesus didn't go right away and Lazarus died. In fact, by the time Jesus reached Bethany, Lazarus had been dead four days. Mary and Martha couldn't understand why he didn't come right away. They knew He could have healed Lazarus."

"He let them down too," Justin said, feeling he could relate to this family.

"I'm sure that's what Mary and Martha thought," Dan agreed. "The Bible tells us Jesus wept when he saw their grief. This family was special to Him, and it hurt Him to see them grieving. But the story doesn't end there. They took Him to see the grave, and Jesus raised Lazarus from the dead. And because of this, many Jews who witnessed the miracle believed on Jesus."

Justin frowned. "What's your point?"

"You see," Dan continued, "If Jesus had healed Lazarus, not as many people would have believed He was the Messiah. But when He raised Lazarus from the grave it left no doubt in their minds. Martha and Mary were hurting, but they got to witness the power of God Almighty through their grieving. God always has a reason for what He does.

"Even God the Father knows how we feel. When Jesus, who was God's only begotten Son, was 33 years old, He was falsely accused of blasphemy and crucified. This was the ultimate plan for our Salvation. Jesus took all the sins of every man, who ever had or ever would live, upon Himself. And God, being perfect, could not look at sin and had to turn away from the Son He dearly loved. Jesus cried out 'My God, my God, why hast thou forsaken me?'"

Justin sank back in his seat. Could God know how he felt? What it was like to watch someone you love die? But why had He done it? He is God after all! And Jesus Himself had felt forsaken?

Dan took a swallow of his water before continuing. "It hurt God for His Son to go through that, but He loved *us* so much, He was willing to let His Son die so we could one day join Them Both in Heaven. After Jesus died, He was buried in a borrowed tomb. He only needed it for three days though, for on the third day, Sunday, He rose from the dead. Salvation's work was completed. He paid for our sins so we don't have to go to hell when we die."

Justin perked up a little. "So, every time something seemed like God didn't care, it was for a greater good?"

"Right! Jesus dying made a way for us to get to heaven and become His 'Brother'. All we have to do is realize we are sinners, believe in our hearts that Jesus is the Son of God, ask Him to forgive us of our sins, and we are saved forever. No one can change that. He did all that for you, for me and everyone ever to walk this earth."

Just at that moment his pager went off.

Chapter 8
Others First

Look not every man on his own things, but every man also on the things of others.
Philippians 2:4

Why now, Dan groaned inwardly as he and his rookie partner were paged to an accident. He turned to Justin. He pulled a tract out of his pocket and handed it to him. "Please read this, and think about what I've said Justin. Your life depends on it." He turned to his partner. "Let's roll!"

Justin took the tract, placed it in his pocket and turned back towards the window, staring at nothing in particular.

Katherine continued serving customers as they came and went, mostly local businessmen as well as several policemen. Glancing out the window, Katherine announced, "The snow's stopped."

Nicole looked up. "Really? How soon do you think the roads will be cleared?"

Katherine narrowed her eyes. "I don't know, it's hard to tell."

"No hurry," Bella remarked. "This place is inspiring! Can I order another Salted Caramel Latté?"

Katherine laughed and took the money handed to her. "Coming right up."

Katherine's cellphone jangled as she handed Bella her latté. She picked up the phone and unlocked the screen to read the text. "Oh! Nicole, come here!"

Nicole popped up from her chair and rushed to the counter. "Oh! Officer Wright's baby! Is it a boy or a girl?"

"It's a boy, Ellis Lee Wright Jr."

They made over the picture and Katherine sent the Wrights her congratulations.

Nicole moved back to her table and was delving deep into her class assignments. Justin was still staring out the window, deep in thought.

The Coffee Shop was quiet for several minutes, the only sounds being gentle music from the radio, the scratch of Nicole's pencil and the clicking of Bella's nails on her computer.

Katherine was coming to the closing chapters of *The Day She Fell*. Her eyes roved over the pages.

He kicked the stubble with the toe of his scuffed shoe. He laughed a sarcastic laugh. Wasn't he the one who once said he would never wear shoes with blemishes? All that was in the first part of his life. That's how he thought of his life before the fall of Paris...the first part. He was now trapped in a horrible second part.

"It'll only look worse if you keep digging it into the cobble stone, Karle," Madeline said, wrapping her scarf around her tighter.

Karle shrugged. "Doesn't matter anymore," he mumbled. He rubbed his hands over his arms. "Terrible cold." He looked at the apartment he had once lived in...now bursting at the seams with German invaders. He spat in the dust on the street. "Bet they aren't in the least cold."

*"I don't care either way," Madeline said, her voice tight. "I care about **us** being cold. Let's hurry to the meeting."*

The two walked briskly down the street towards the Café Paris. Natalia had said to be there at 4:00 on the dot and they would just make it.

They weren't disappointed. Dominique motioned with his thumb towards the pantry door as they entered. They slipped through the doorway and moved the loose portion of flooring, dropping noiselessly into the cellar meeting place.

That chapter ended, with only two left, but Katherine would have to read them later. *Bella is such a talented author,* she mused. *If only she would give her talent to God...*

Another customer entered the shop. It was Lisa, a friend from church. She and Katherine taught a Sunday school class together. "Merry Christmas, Lisa! What are you doing out on a day like this? Aren't the roads still blocked?" Katherine asked.

Lisa flashed a bright smile. "They're clear as far as my house, in town anyway. I need to pick up some of your delicious Chocolate Chip Cookies for a gathering tonight. I haven't the time to bake any with all the other cooking I'm doing today!"

"I understand," Katherine said with a grin. "I've got two dozen fresh. Will that be enough?"

"Just right," Lisa sighed, pulling out her wallet. Katherine turned to package the cookies.

"You know, Kath, I've been trying to come up with a meaningful way to do this week's Sunday School lesson."

"What? About selfishness? I thought it should have been lined up before Christmas personally."

Lisa nodded. "I know! It would have been easier then! But we can't change it now. Any ideas?"

Katherine subconsciously drummed her fingers on the table. "You know, Lisa, you could talk about how the Christmas season is surrounded by selfishness, but how The One who came was the perfect example of unselfishness. Ask them to put themselves in Jesus' place. He had everything, but gave it up to be born on earth and one day die. Most of the time

He is ignored. Ask them if they would have done the same thing if they had been Jesus. Get them to thinking."

"Then you could address the Christian life. Life for a servant of God is not to be lived for ourselves. We shouldn't make a decision without asking God first. We should take even the smallest things to God."

Lisa nodded, pondering what Katherine had said. "And that would give you a springboard for the next lesson on serving others."

"Right!" agreed Katherine.

"I was thinking the other day about making decisions," Lisa continued. "It seems no matter what we do, we're affecting someone else's plans, either for the good or the bad. We have to choose if we're going to be self-serving or take others into consideration."

Katherine nodded eagerly. "Can I borrow that for my lesson?"

Lisa laughed. "No, it's copy-written!" Katherine grinned as Lisa said, "Of course you can use it. I'm taking your outline, aren't I?"

Gently touching Katherine's arm, she asked, "How are you getting along today?"

Bella and Nicole looked up as Katherine replied, "I'm missing him something terrible, but God is helping me through it." Tears shown in her eyes as she said, "I can't believe he's been gone a year now."

Lisa came around the counter and hugged her friend. "We've all been praying for you today. I knew it would be especially hard for you. If there's anything we can do, please call us."

"I will, thank you, Lisa."

Bella glanced at Nicole, who seemed to understand exactly what was wrong. *Okay, probably her husband,* Bella thought. Nicole was looking at the police display and the picture of Mr. Shannon. Bella's stomach twisted. Not only was Mr. Shannon a policeman, he was a fallen officer!

62

Lisa glanced at her watch. "Oh! I need to get back to the house! I left Jason in charge and he's probably about to pull his hair out!" she said, referring to her seventeen year old son.

"I'll see you at church," Katherine said, wiping her eyes. "Merry Christmas to you and yours!"

"Merry Christmas!" Lisa called over her shoulder.

Katherine busied herself with some dishes in the kitchen. Though the conversation between Katherine and Lisa hadn't been loud, Nicole couldn't help but overhear it...and feel stabs of conviction.

Others first, she thought. The letter inviting her to the college in Europe danced in her mind's eye. Was she thinking of others by deciding to accept it?

She recalled a comment her mother had made to her father. "I don't know how I'll be able to manage with Nicole gone. I'm barely able to keep things going with her at a community college! If she goes abroad, I'll be lost!"

Father had nodded and said, "I'm worried about her going over there alone...but I don't want to ruin her dream...I just can't get peace on whether it's best for her. I know the church will have to scramble for a pianist. No one else knows how to play the piano that well."

Nicole squirmed in her chair there at *The Coffee Shop*, her papers and assignments forgotten. Her siblings would have a tougher load to shoulder with her gone. And she'd also be knocking her sister Jennifer out of getting to go on a mission's trip. The only way she could go next year was if Nicole went with her...and she would already be gone.

Guilt nagged at her conscience. She'd not once prayed about whether she should go or not. It was her dream come true after all...but what if it were actually a temptation to get her to stray from her walk with the Lord?

Deep in the innermost parts of her heart, Nicole knew this wasn't at all what God had wanted for her. At one point in her life, she had known what His will was...to be a keeper at home, helping her mother, giving her piano talent to God, maybe teaching some lessons. For her, college wasn't even part of His plan at all. That had been her own desire…and by taking her own path, she had strayed so far as to take a part-time job on campus to help cover her classes…classes she hadn't even prayed about taking.

She held her head in her hands. Why hadn't she checked with Him first?

Nicole set her jaw. She knew why. Someone had said she had more talent than she gave herself credit for. It had turned her head. And slowly began her downward spiral toward self-gratification.

Perhaps she should change her course…get back to what God wanted for her. But she would be giving up everything she had dreamed of! All her ambitions…her opportunity…her name in the archives of Musical History…

Her thoughts were interrupted by the distinct sound of a snowplow.

Chapter 9
Saying Goodbye

Come now, and let us reason together, saith the LORD: though your sins be as scarlet, they shall be as white as snow; though they be red like crimson, they shall be as wool.
Isaiah 1:18

Nicole turned around in her chair to see the welcome sight of the state snowplow at work, effortlessly pushing the soft flakes down the road and into an alleyway. She sighed and smiled. "Guess I'll be heading home soon." She turned and packed her papers back into her messenger bag.

Katherine laid aside her book. "Appears that way. I must say, this place will seem out and out lonely once y'all leave!"

"Well, you'll see me again at church, Mrs. Shannon," Nicole said brightly. Glancing at the others, she said, "I can't vouch for these two, though."

Hope I never come back here, Justin thought. It was nice for a day, but he was sure glad he didn't live there.

Bella looked up from her typing. "I doubt I'll be in this area again…I was only here because I missed my flight to my friend's place. But I must say, this has been charming!" Her fingers never broke pace with her work.

Katherine busied herself in the kitchen area for several minutes. When she returned, Justin watched her place a few things under the counter.

About fifteen minutes later, Deputy Kyle Pickett entered the shop. "Good news, folks! The roads are clear now! The white stuff was fluffy and easy to clear. The roadblock's down and you can continue on your way!"

Justin stood and limped to the counter as Deputy Pickett left. "Thank you for your hospitality, Mrs. Shannon."

"Not at all. Thank you again for your service, and Merry Christmas." She pulled a small sack of cookies from under the counter. "I stuck the last of the, um, 'well-done' cookies in there, but I put some fresh ones in as well."

"You didn't have to do that," Justin protested.

"I know, but I want to." She turned and poured him a to-go cup of coffee. "Have a wonderful time with your nieces and nephew!"

Justin offered her a slight smile. "Thank you, Mrs. Shannon." He paused for a moment, then forced the words out of his mouth, "Merry Christmas." He limped toward the door, then outside to his parked truck.

Nicole hoisted her bag onto her shoulder. "Thanks for letting me camp out here, Mrs. Shannon! Merry Christmas!"

"Merry Christmas," Katherine called, coming around to open the door for the girl. She handed Nicole a baggie of cookies. "Enjoy!"

"Thank you so much! You're the best!" she said as she gave Katherine a hug.

The door swung shut and Katherine turned back towards Bella. "Are you going to abandon me too?"

Bella smiled a reserved sort of smile. "Not yet. This place is so inspiring...I can't get over it. I wish I could move your shop to New York! I could *really* write novels here! And your Lattés are awesome!"

"Well thank you," Katherine laughed. "Do you like salted caramel that much?"

"Oh, *Yes*! I love them! In fact, could I get another?"

Katherine laughed harder. "You sure can. But I'll cover this one. Merry Christmas."

"Oh, thank you." Bella studied Katherine for a moment. "You are such a sweet person, Mrs. Shannon. No wonder people here love this place. The world needs more people like you in it."

Katherine smiled and walked over with the latté. "Thank you for saying so, but believe me, Katherine Shannon has her faults like everyone else."

Bella laughed softly. "No one is perfect, I suppose." She stirred her drink, her brow creased. "Mrs. Shannon, I overheard what that woman said to you earlier. I assumed she meant your husband had passed away...please accept my condolences."

Katherine nodded. "Thank you, Bella. I appreciate it."

They were silent for a moment. Then Bella said, "You were talking about Christmas earlier. What *do* you believe about Christmas?"

Katherine pulled out a chair from the next table and sat down. "Well, I believe Christmas is meant to celebrate the birth of Jesus Christ."

Bella leaned back in her chair and folded her arms. "Tell me about it. I've never heard the whole story."

Katherine stared at her, her mouth opening, but no words leaving her. *How sad!* Finding her voice, she said, "Well, let me read you some scriptures about it." She reached into her apron pocket and pulled out a New Testament.

"In Luke chapter 1, starting in verse 26 it says, *And in the sixth month the angel Gabriel was sent from God unto a city of Galilee, named Nazareth,*

"*To a virgin espoused to a man whose name was Joseph, of the house of David; and the virgin's name was Mary.*

"*And the angel came in unto her, and said, Hail, thou that art highly favoured, the Lord is with thee: blessed art thou among women.*

"And when she saw him, she was troubled at his saying, and cast in her mind what manner of salutation this should be.

"And the angel said unto her, Fear not, Mary: for thou hast found favour with God.

"And, behold, thou shalt conceive in thy womb, and bring forth a son, and shalt call his name JESUS.

"He shall be great, and shall be called the Son of the Highest: and the Lord God shall give unto him the throne of his father David:

"And he shall reign over the house of Jacob for ever; and of his kingdom there shall be no end.

"Then said Mary unto the angel, How shall this be, seeing I know not a man?

"And the angel answered and said unto her, The Holy Ghost shall come upon thee, and the power of the Highest shall overshadow thee: therefore also that holy thing which shall be born of thee shall be called the Son of God...

"And picking up with verse 37, *For with God nothing shall be impossible.*

"And Mary said, Behold the handmaid of the Lord; be it unto me according to thy word. And the angel departed from her."

"So are you one of those people who believes we should pray to Mary and all that?" Bella asked, marked skepticism in her voice.

"Certainly not," Katherine said, a flush stealing over her face. "Mary was a good girl, but just like the rest of us, she was a sinner. The only Man who walked in human flesh and never sinned was the Baby she carried, Jesus Christ."

Katherine turned the page to Luke chapter 2. Skimming the verses, she explained the story. "Around the time Mary was to give birth, Caesar Augustus declared all the world should be taxed. Joseph, now Mary's husband, took Mary and returned to the city of his birth, Bethlehem, according to the decree.

"When they arrived in Bethlehem, there was no room for them in the inn, which is like a hotel. But they were able to take shelter in a stable…"

"A stable? You mean she *really* had the baby in a barn?" Bella asked. She shook her head. "How disgusting! And if He is the Son of God, why wasn't He at least born in a house?"

Katherine smiled and calmly replied, "To fulfill the promises God had made about His Son, and so no one could ever say Jesus grew up in the lap of luxury. He was born into a poor family. And unlike most children these days, He was raised to work. The Bible tells us He was a carpenter.

"But back to the story, Mary did have Him in the stable, wrapping Him in swaddling clothes and laid Him in a manger." Katherine grinned as Bella shuddered.

"And He had special guests that night. On the hills, a group of shepherds were watching over their flocks of sheep. An angel appeared to them and told them, *'Fear not: for, behold, I bring you good tidings of great joy, which shall be to all people. For unto you is born this day in the city of David a Saviour, which is Christ the Lord. And this shall be a sign unto you; Ye shall find the babe wrapped in swaddling clothes, lying in a manger.'*

"The Bible tells us, *'And suddenly there was with the angel a multitude of the heavenly host praising God, and saying, Glory to God in the highest, and on earth peace, good will toward men.'*"

"Okay, so we're talking smelly guys on a hillside? *They* are the ones who get this special message from God?" Bella shook her head. "This is *so* twisted! I mean, Jesus, according to you, was like a Prince or something and shepherds are the ones that…agh!"

Katherine smiled. "Does seem odd doesn't it? But the Bible refers to Jesus as the Good Shepherd, and one of His ancestors, King David, started out as a shepherd. It's symbolic of Who Jesus is and that He came to help the lowly as well as those of high regard."

"What about those king looking guys you always see in the Nativities?" Bella asked, pointing to the main Nativity on the counter.

"They actually came about two years later. They are called 'Wisemen' in the Bible and came from the east. They brought gifts to toddler Jesus of gold, frankincense and myrrh."

Bella nodded sharply. "Now that's more like it!"

Katherine laughed. "Yes, they knew Who Jesus was."

"I've always wondered, but I've never known anyone I felt comfortable enough to ask this question." Katherine nodded and Bella continued, "Why did He come?"

Katherine had been waiting for this. "He came to die for the sins of all men."

"That's the part I don't get, the dying part. Why would He?"

"Because He loves us. It says in John 3:16, *'For God so loved the world, that he gave his only begotten Son, that whosoever believeth in him should not perish, but have everlasting life.'* He sent His son to die for us so we could one day live with Him in heaven..."

Katherine shared the gospel with Bella, watching her expressions of indignation over the treatment Jesus received leading up to His crucifixion.

"And He said nothing? He let them mock Him, spit in His face, beat Him up and whip Him and said *nothing?*"

"Nothing. He suffered all of that silently for us..." She told Bella of His death. Bella could see it all, Jesus, covered in blood, writhing in agony on a rough wooden cross, crying out to God, asking why His Father had forsaken Him. She could see, and hate, the soldiers and people mocking this Innocent Man and casting lots for His garments. She could imagine the intense grief His mother and His followers were experiencing. She could smell the blood and sweat...feel the change in the air and the fear that swept over the crowd as darkness overtook the sky.

By instinct, Bella reached for her notepad and pen. She had to get this down on paper. This was a compelling story.

But Bella couldn't seem to get anything written down. She sat frozen, hanging on every word. Something told her *this* story was different.

Katherine told her of Christ's rising from the dead three days later. Bella subconsciously released her breath. If the story had ended before this, she would have died!

Katherine went in for the big question. "Bella, wouldn't you like for Him to take your sins away? After all He's done for you, don't you think you can trust Him with your life and love Him?"

Bella shifted her gaze away. Trying to sound like her professional self, she said, "I didn't ask Him to die for me. This is all new to me…"

Katherine leaned forward. "You're absolutely right about that, Bella. It would be new, completely new. A new life, a new birth, a new way of thinking."

"It's a lot to consider. I'll think about it Mrs. Shannon."

She turned back to her laptop. Katherine's shoulders dropped, worry lines etching her forehead. "Don't put it off, Bella."

Bella nodded to Katherine. "I *will* think about it, Mrs. Shannon. I promise."

Katherine slowly made her way back to the counter. *Lord, draw her to You,* she pleaded with her Savior.

Half an hour later, Bella packed her laptop up. She approached the counter where Katherine was about to finish *The Day She Fell.* "It's been a pleasure meeting you, Mrs. Shannon. I fear I have to leave now, but I want you to know, this is the best Christmas Eve I've had in a long time."

Katherine stood and shook Bella's outstretched hand. "I can honestly say the same. I hope we will see each other again…and I'll keep my eyes open for your books. You're a talented young woman, Bella. Please remember what we've talked about and give your talent back to the One Who gave it to you."

Bella nodded slowly as she said, "I will seriously consider it."

Katherine handed her a sack of cookies and a John/Romans booklet. "Merry Christmas, Bella."

"Merry Christmas, Mrs. Shannon."

Bella glanced up at the picture of Bryson as she turned toward the door. She slowed her pace, thinking. Then, decidedly, she approached the trashcan and with a rapid motion ripped two stickers off of her travel bag, tossing them in. And with that Bella left the shop.

Katherine silently prayed for the girl. She straightened up the shop a bit. A few customers trickled in and out as the afternoon progressed.

That evening, she closed up her shop, gave the remaining soup to Deputy Pickett and drove home. Her evening was filled with Christmas preparations, making food and wrapping the last few gifts. She laid out Bella's card to give to her grandmother in her next letter.

That night, she sat on the couch to finish reading Bella's book.

Madeline stared at Natalia in utter bewilderment. "What are you saying, girl? What does it all mean?"

Natalia's breath was shaky. "It means simply this, Madeline. He's gone. The Germans have arrested him. And I fear they will...that they will execute him for his part in the Résistance."

A muffled scream escaped Madeline's lips. "NO! Oh, you're lying!"

"I wish I was, Madeline."

Madeline reeled back, away from her friend, holding her head. She was dizzy, sick to her stomach and she couldn't get her breath. "No...not..." she choked. Natalia rushed forward to console her friend. Madeline pushed her away. "Not Karle! Not Karle too!"

Katherine turned the page, her heart nearly in her throat, worried about her second favorite character. Her eyes snapped. The page was blank. "What? No! You can't leave me hanging like that!"

Chapter 10
Merry Christmas

Therefore, my beloved brethren, be ye stedfast, unmoveable, always abounding in the work of the Lord, forasmuch as ye know that your labour is not in vain in the Lord.
1 Corinthians 15:58

Katherine laid her purse and Bible on the counter as she came in from church the next day. She hurried about the kitchen, getting out food and checking crock pots.

"Door's open," she called in answer to Dan's knock.

"Merry Christmas, Aunt Kate!" said little Marie, running up to hug Katherine. Katherine hugged her back. Even though they had all attended church together that morning, the youngster didn't let that stop her from calling out the greeting over and over.

"Merry Christmas to you too! Would you like to help Anna set the table?"

The four year old bobbed her head up and down and hurried to help her eight year old sister. Jeff came in, laden with packages. "Where do you want these, Aunt Kate?"

"Just put them on the sofa in the living room, will you?"

"Yes, ma'am."

Isabelle bustled in and hugged her sister before donning her own apron. "Put me to work, sis!"

Katherine grinned at her younger sister. "Can you handle the creamed potatoes?"

"Sure thing."

"And Dan," Katherine said with a flattering tone, "I was hoping I could impose upon my big strong brother-in-law to carve the roast for his favorite sister-in-law?"

Dan grinned. "Only if I get to taste-test!"

"Never mind," she said, her shoulders falling before the trio of adults burst into laughter. Katherine handed him the knife and left him to work his wonders on her savory roast beef.

Eleven year old Janie practically flew into the room, her red braids dancing behind her. "Aunt Kate! There's a man at the door asking for you and I don't know who he is!"

"Nothing to be worried about," called Dylan, thirteen. "Dad, it's that policeman that was on the news yesterday. The one that got hurt."

Katherine dried her hands. "Cpl. Ericson? He's supposed to be in South Carolina." She took off her apron and hurried to the door, Dan and four of the seven kids close behind her.

Sure enough, Justin stood in the door way, a ball cap in his hands. He nodded as Katherine greeted him. "Merry Christmas, Mrs. Shannon, Sgt. Piper. I suppose I owe you an apology for dropping in like this, unannounced."

"Oh, Janie 'denounced' you," Max, Marie's twin, assured him.

Justin half smiled at this remark. "I'm heading down to South Carolina, but I stopped by the department, hoping to talk to Dan and they told me he was over here. They gave me directions. I hope that's alright."

Katherine replied, "Of course! That's fine." She turned to Dan. "Y'all can use the study." Dan turned toward the kids, who instantly scampered off to the kitchen.

"Oh, that's not necessary," Justin said. "It'll only take a minute and I've got to get on the road."

"Here, we'll just step outside," Dan said, following Justin out.

"It's really nothing big, just wanted to return this," he said, shoving a piece of paper into Dan's hand. "You left that on the table yesterday. I read it, but I'm done with it now. Thought you might want it back."

Dan glanced down at the tract Justin had given him. "Justin, you weren't supposed to-"

"Hey, I figured you'd rather have it back than for me to throw it away. I'd like to stay around, but I've got to get going if I'm gonna get to South Carolina before it gets any later. See ya' around."

Dan stood on the porch, watching as Justin pulled out of the driveway. *God, please work in his heart!* Slowly, Dan turned and entered the house, just in time to overhear the boys talking.

"What do you think he wants?" Jeff whispered to Dylan.

The older boy shrugged as he set the bread on the table. "Maybe he's asking dad about a lawyer or something. You know he's under investigation."

"Dylan," Isabelle scolded. "That's enough."

"Sorry."

Katherine wiped her hands on a towel. "Well, that's all until dessert. I suppose we could fix the little ones' plates and if Dan isn't finished by then, they can go ahead and start."

Isabelle nodded, then caught sight of Dan standing in the doorway. His head was down, the sparkle gone from his eyes. "What's wrong, honey?"

Dan shook his head and held up the tract. "He returned it. He said...that he was done with it."

Katherine frowned and took the tract. "I'm sorry, Dan."

"I just don't understand! He seemed so ready when I got finished talking with him yesterday! If only that dumb pager hadn't gone off..."

"Uh, Dan," Katherine said, holding out the tract, "Could this be why he gave it back?"

Dan took the tract, staring at the back page. At the bottom were Justin's name, address and yesterday's date. Dan scanned the type above it. "If you have prayed the Sinner's prayer with a sincere heart and have asked Jesus to save you, please fill out the information below and return it to us! We look forward to hearing from you!"

Dan blinked and looked up at his wife and sister-in-law. "He did it! He actually did it! Oh, Praise God!"

"That's the best present we could have gotten," Isabelle said, hugging her husband and sister all at once.

Tears welled in Katherine's eyes; happy tears. As they blessed the food and engaged in the usual Christmas conversations, Katherine silently thanked God. *You answered my prayer. You gave me work to do yesterday. And already, we get to see the fruit. Lord, help me be ever ready to speak a word for You. And thank You for allowing me to run* The Coffee Shop. *Thank You for reassuring me that I'm exactly where I belong. And thank You for the reminder that I just needed to be still and know that You are God.*

Work in Bella's heart, Lord. Let her see her need of You in her life. Protect her and draw her to You, Father.

"Open your present, Aunt Katie!" Marie begged, plopping a heavy package on Katherine's lap.

"Alrighty, Marie. Would you like to help?" Needing no second invitation, Marie pulled the wrapping off. Katherine nearly squealed like a girl. She held in her lap Bella's French Résistance trilogy.

She grabbed the second book, and quickly flipped through it. She sighed with relief. Though not one for spoilers, she just couldn't bring herself to wait and see if Karle was rescued. Katherine hugged the children. "Thank you so much. I'll enjoy these, I know!"

As Katherine watched her nieces and nephews unwrap their gifts that afternoon, she had no idea that at the Hanover home, Nicole had announced to her family she wasn't going to

Europe to study. She didn't know Bella had, for the first time in her life, attended a church service that morning. Only God knew where this would lead.

But she did know one thing. *The Coffee Shop* was staying open. She glanced at Bryson's picture hanging next to the Christmas tree. Peace flooded her heart. *I love you, Bryson.*

Katherine got to her feet and returned to the kitchen, calling over her shoulder, "Coffee anyone?"

The End

My Testimony

In September 2001, 9/11 took place. I was five years old, and I remember people talking about the planes flying into the Twin Towers. I didn't understand what was going on, but it scared me. When I heard about all those people dying, it set me to thinking about where I would go after I died.

On July 3rd, 2002, when I was six, my sister Gera and I were playing David and Goliath in our backyard. Dad was grilling in preparation for America's birthday the following day. Different things from sermons I'd heard came to my mind, and I began asking dad some questions. To be honest, I don't remember what the exact questions were, but I do remember that they had to do with Salvation.

Dad answered my questions to my satisfaction, and I went back to play, but the conviction of the Holy Spirit compelled me to settle the question of my eternity that day. I knelt next to my mom's flower garden and asked the Lord to forgive me of my sins and save me. I have never regretted that decision.

It is my prayer this book would be a witness to the lost and a challenge to the Christian to get out there and be a witness to others.

One last thank you to all those who are serving or have served as United States Policemen. You are a big part of keeping this Nation safe. Thank you for your service!

May God Bless You!
Writing for HIM,

Ryana Lynn Miller

Other Books By Ryana Lynn!
Available at www.lifeofheritage.com!

The Land of Cotton
1861
Our Home in Dixieland
Book One in The Battle for Heritage Series

The Land of Cotton is a story of two strong wills: the will of man and the will of God. Watch how each is played out in hearts and lives both on and off the battlefield.

> *"You mean to tell me that you plan to lead part of this family into this rebellion? Don't think that this only affects you, Silas. You married my daughter and this affects all of us!"*

Join the Masons, an ordinary family living during as extraordinary time in our nation's history, the Civil War. See them challenged to do some extraordinary things while seeking the will of God. Read History on almost every page as the Masons realize God has a time for everything…even war! (Ecclesiastes 3:8)

This book that the whole family will enjoy has a two-fold challenge in it: meet the Savior and know Him well, and study your history and know it well.

Our Heritage to Save
1862
Our Fight for Freedom
Book Two in The Battle for Heritage Series

Heritage. Family. Freedom. What would you be willing to do to protect them? This is the question that the soldiers of the Blue and the Gray asked themselves multiple times no doubt during the War Between the States. And the Mason family is not exempt from answering it.

"I have sons fighting in both armies, and that is not acceptable to me. My younger son chose his...his 'country' over his family."
Seth's eyes were sincere as he slowly said, "Hard decisions have to be made in time of war, sir. I have cousins in the Union army as well. You're right, it hurts. It hurts my mama a lot, because she's from up north. But the rights of life, liberty and property must be defended."

Join the Masons as they enter the second year of conflict between the Confederacy and the Union. As loyalties are tested, some soldiers must choose between their beliefs and their families. Be reminded that war is not all glory, but also a good deal of anxiety, sorrow and broken dreams.

May the whole family enjoy this story as they seek a closer relationship with the Lord and learn more about our Nation's history.

Please tune in...

The Fundamental Broadcasting Network
fbnradio.com
A local church ministry of Grace Baptist Church
in Newport, North Carolina

FBN offers:
- ✓ King James only Preaching
- ✓ Conservative Christian Music
- ✓ Short Devotionals
- ✓ Dramatizations and Cantatas
- ✓ Preachers and Singers of the Past and Present and much, much more!

You won't have to worry about something inappropriate coming into your home with this radio station! We have been heard in all 50 states and in over 220 countries! We also have a children's site, fbnkids.com!

How Can You Listen?
- ✓ By Internet: fbnradio.com
- ✓ By Free Apps for Apple and Android devices
- ✓ Livestream by Phone: 605-781-9840
- ✓ By Radio: Check our Website for a list of all of our 40+ stations and see if we have one in your area, or write/call FBN for a free program guide.

520 Roberts Rd.
Newport, NC 28570
252-223-4600

We Would Love to Hear From You!